THE PATIO
CLUB®

WRITTEN AND ILLUSTRATED BY

CARYN MOTTILLA

I0550623

Julie's July Picnic

Julie's July Picnic
The Patio Club ®
Published by Open Window Publishing
Castle Rock, CO

Publisher's Cataloging-in-Publication data

Names: Mottilla, Caryn, author.
Title: Julie's July Picnic / by Caryn Mottilla.
Description: First trade paperback original edition. Also available as an ebook. | Castle Rock [Colorado] : Open Window Publishing, 2019. | Series: The Patio Club.
Identifiers: ISBN 978-0-9997471-8-8
Subjects: LCSH: Old age—Fiction. | Month of July—Fiction. | Aging parents—Fiction. | Short stories.
BISAC: FICTION / General.
Classification: LCC PS374.O43 | DDC 813—dc22

Cover design by Caryn Mottilla

QUANTITY PURCHASES: Schools, companies, professional groups, clubs, and other organizations may qualify for special terms when ordering quantities of this title. For information, email ThePatioClub@gmail.com.

OPEN WINDOW
PUBLISHING

The Patio Club® is dedicated to the men and women in assisted living communities, memory and Hospice care who have listened to the adventures of The Patio Club®. They expressed their hope for these stories to be published and shared with others across the country.

Introducing the Patio Club

The Patio Club was originally formed by two sets of sisters—
Elaine and Adele from New Jersey, and Betty and Mildred from
Kentucky. The women were young when they met in the 1940s.
The years passed by, and later in life, the four adventurous women
made a pact that after they died they would meet up and visit
retirement and assisted living communities. After they passed
away, they came to Happy Visions Retirement Home and liked it
so much they decided to stay.

The women call themselves "The Patio Club," because they sit
outside on the patio of Happy Visions. Each day, Elaine, Adele,

Betty and Mildred are surrounded by colorful sparkles, and they meet a steady stream of interesting visitors and residents who pass through Happy Visions on their way to unknown destinations.

One amazing thing is that the Patio Club can look to the sky and watch a video of each person's life. This precious gift lets the Patio Club understand the unique story that each person carries with them.

Julie's July Picnic

THE HEAT OF EARLY JULY WHISPERED IN THE warm breeze that blew softly through the hallways of Happy Visions Retirement Home. The windows were open and the staff and residents felt the heat more than usual because the air-conditioning was being repaired. To stay cool, residents wore damp towels around their necks

The women of the Patio Club sat in the back yard in the cool grass under the oak tree. "When will they fix the air-conditioning?" asked Betty. Then she laughed and said, "It's hard to believe I did not have air-conditioning until

I had been married almost thirty years. Now, it's hard to imagine being without it."

Adele smiled. "Most of the residents grew up without air-conditioning. I bet they have a few tricks up their sleeves to stay cool until it's repaired."

Inside of Happy Visions, in the memory care unit, a woman named Julie sat by the window, watching squirrels playing in the oak tree. She did this each day, regardless of the month or the weather.

Julie had soft blue eyes and curly, gray hair. Her happy nature made her seem years younger than her real age.

A young woman named Amanda was Julie's caretaker. She stood quietly beside her and wiped Julie's face and hands with a fresh washcloth.

Suddenly, Julie said, "It's a great day for a July picnic! They are the best! I am going to make baked beans, barbeque, potato salad and vanilla cupcakes with strawberry icing. Remember, no one may eat the picnic

food until after they play volleyball. A July picnic is not the same without a good volleyball game."

Amanda listened, as she did each day, as Julie talked about picnics in July. "Will you play volleyball this year, Julie?" asked Amanda. "When I look outside, though, I don't see a volleyball net."

"Don't you worry," said Julie. "By tomorrow morning, there will be a volleyball net and a red, white and blue volleyball for the game."

Outside, Elaine happened to look in the window and saw Julie with Amanda. "There's Julie," said Elaine to Adele, Betty and Mildred. "She's always so happy. Every day, she sits at her window and watches the squirrels climb the oak tree."

Mildred waved to Julie as she spoke to Elaine. "Have you ever talked to Julie? I have. She loves July picnics and volleyball. In fact, that is the only memory she has now. She is in her late seventies, and that one memory visits

her each day. Julie always says no one can eat the picnic food at her July picnic until after the volleyball game!"

Elaine, Adele and Betty were amused by the idea of requiring guests to play volleyball in order to partake of the picnic food. "What a great idea," said Adele. "Do you think people actually played volleyball before they ate?"

Elaine laughed and said, "Probably so. I hear she has vivid memories of those volleyball games."

Later that same afternoon, the women of the Patio Club walked inside where the temperature was much warmer than usual. They watched as Amanda, the caretaker, hung an invitation on the cork bulletin board in the dining area.

Mildred smiled and asked Amanda, "What is this invitation? It says, 'Julie's July Volleyball Game and Picnic?'"

Amanda giggled. She was young with long, blond hair tied back in a ponytail. Amanda always had a smile and a hug for residents. She often wore colorful shirts with

cartoon animals to entertain the residents in memory care. Her happy attitude and great sense of humor brought joy to many of the residents.

"Oh, this is a *very* special invitation," said Amanda. "I told Julie we are going to have 'Julie's July Volleyball Game and Picnic.' We aren't *really* having a full-length, official volleyball game. However, Julie has a rule that we can't eat the picnic food until *after* the volleyball game. So, we're playing a token game just so we can eat."

Adele looked over the invitation. She smiled as she read it to Elaine, Betty and Mildred.

"Join us tomorrow for Julie's July Volleyball Game and Picnic. Residents will play volleyball *before* the picnic. Julie has promised to lead her team to an early victory. This will be followed by a picnic on the patio. Hotdogs, barbeque, potato salad and cupcakes will be served."

"Wait a minute," said Adele. "Do the residents know they will be playing volleyball in this July heat?" Mildred laughed at Adele's reaction and so did Elaine and Betty.

Amanda answered, "I've worked at Happy Visions for five years and stranger things have happened here." Then she winked and walked down the hallway.

"Adele," said Mildred. "It's ridiculous to think the residents would *ever* play volleyball even if it was cold in July. But maybe this one time, we can get the residents to play for Julie."

"Wait a minute," Betty said. "Let's go outside and see what the video in the sky reveals to us. Maybe we can see why July volleyball picnics hold such special meaning for Julie."

The women of the Patio Club walked through the grass past the shade of the tall oak tree. As they looked to the sky, the video began to play.

It showed a girl around eight years old who looked like Julie. She jumped with excitement as she asked her mom, "Will our guests play volleyball with me the day of the July picnic?"

"I don't know," said Julie's mom as she wiped her hands on her apron. It was decorated with picnic tables. "You'll have to ask them."

Julie replied, "I don't think we should let anyone eat the picnic food until they play volleyball with me." Julie's mom laughed at her young daughter's remark.

The video continued and showed the day of the picnic. It was a hot day in July that year. Julie gave her directions to the guests. "In order to eat, you have to play volleyball with me." Guests were laughing as they walked to the volleyball net Julie's father had set up in the backyard. After the guests assembled in the grass, Julie hit the ball over the net as people cheered."

Julie tired quickly of the game as most young children do. She turned to the guests and said, "Ok. Now you can eat the picnic food." Many of the guests were still laughing as they walked to the nearby picnic tables. The food Julie's mom and neighbors had made was waiting for them.

The video continued and the years passed by quickly. Julie was now married. She wore her mother's old apron as she stood in her own kitchen speaking to her newest neighbor, Polly. "I grew up as an only child. Each July, I always host a July volleyball game and picnic just like my parents did when I was a child. People laugh at me, but my rule is no one can eat until we play volleyball. My guests humor me and play. What's a good picnic without volleyball?"

The video suddenly ended. The women of the Patio Club noticed Amanda had joined them. "You may not know this," said Amanda, "but Julie dreams of July picnics and volleyball games almost every night. When I go in to check on her, I often hear her in her sleep laughing as she says, 'No one eats till we play volleyball.'"

Betty said, "I think we need to honor Julie's wish and play volleyball. What can it hurt? If the residents knew they just needed to let Julie hit the ball, I bet they would play."

The following morning, Julie looked out her window. Elaine, Adele, Betty and Mildred had just finished putting up a small volleyball net they found in a storage closet. Lying on the ground near the net was a red, white and blue volleyball. On the patio, picnic tables were covered in red and white plastic tablecloths.

"I can't believe we didn't get caught putting up the net," said Betty. "Wait until the residents find out they *have* to play volleyball before they can eat the picnic food!"

Elaine said, "I know a few of them will stand on the court to play. Julie is definitely going to enjoy hitting the ball a few times. Remember, no one eats until Julie hits the ball over the net at least once."

Residents saw the invitation to Julie's picnic on the cork bulletin board. Several of the residents sat at breakfast dressed in bright colors and sneakers. They spoke with excitement at the idea of playing volleyball as well as being a part of making Julie's dream for a July picnic come true.

Around eleven o'clock, before it got *too* hot, residents began standing in place near the volleyball net. Julie watched through her window as people assembled. Suddenly, she stood and pointed to the volleyball net. She cheered with delight and said to Amanda, "This *really is* a July volleyball game and picnic!"

Amanda said, "Would you like to go outside to the picnic?" Julie enthusiastically nodded her head, excited by Amanda's official invitation to go to the picnic. Amanda took Julie's hand and led her outside to the volleyball net. The faded and worn net stood in the shade provided by the shadow of the oak tree.

Residents applauded as Julie approached them. Then Amanda led Julie to her place in the back row to serve the ball. Julie surprised everyone as she spoke and said, "This is just like I remember July picnics in my dreams. Remember, no one eats the picnic food, until we play volleyball!"

In her haste to go outside, Julie was still wearing her bright red, cotton slippers. They seemed like the perfect shoes for volleyball. Amanda reached down and picked up the volleyball. She stood behind Julie and threw the volleyball into the air. Several people on the other side of the net hollered, "Come on Julie! Hit the ball to us!"

The first attempt Julie made to hit the ball did not go well. Her arm and hand took a swing at the ball, but she completely missed! A look of defeat crossed Julie's face. Amanda faced Julie and quietly encouraged her, "Remember, Julie, no one can eat the picnic food until *you* hit the ball over the net."

It may have been the wind or Julie's new-found determination, but Amanda threw the ball again and this time Julie easily hit it *over* the top of the net. No one touched the ball, and Julie scored a *real* point in the volleyball game!

All of the residents along with the women of the Patio Club cheered wildly for a surprised Julie. "It really is like my dreams," she said. "Now everyone can eat!"

"It's hard to believe that's all it took," said Mildred. "One throw of the volleyball and one hit over the net. It's amazing how little it takes for a dream to really come true."

As the residents sat eating, they told stories of July picnics from long ago. Some shared their favorite recipes and others talked of picnic leftovers that lasted for days afterwards.

The women of the Patio Club invited the maintenance crew to the picnic as well. They had fixed the air-conditioning just in time to attend the picnic. Before they ate, several of the workers played volleyball. They had been told Julie's rule that no one could eat until they played volleyball.

As the residents retired inside to the comforts of air-conditioning, Elaine, Adele, Betty and Mildred looked one last time to the video in the sky. It showed Julie years before as she stood in her doctor's office. Her doctor told her she was having memory problems. Julie made

everyone laugh when she said, "No matter what I forget, I will *always* remember July volleyball games and picnics. They are unforgettable."

This July, may you be as delighted as Julie by summer fun and picnics with friends. And, remember Julie's rule: *"You have to play before you can eat!"*

With Love from the Patio Club,

The End.

The Patio Club's Story

IN NOVEMBER OF 2016, I began writing fictional stories for retirement and assisted living communities. This occurred because of a simple request from an older gentleman in his 80s who asked if I could write a story about people "their age." Writing and telling stories has always come easily to me. I happily said, "yes." I was excited at the challenge and have written a story each month since then. They are about a fictional retirement/assisted living community named *Happy Visions*. Each month I read to retirement and assisted living communities. The joy of doing this is overwhelming.

In July of 2017, I was reading to a group of older women as they sat outside *on the patio* in the shade. The women's ages reached up to 95. When I left the patio that day, I decided at that moment to write a story for them called "The Patio Club." The series began with that story.

The stories I write come effortlessly to me. It is as if I am divinely inspired. As I began writing the first story in the Patio Club series, I was so surprised as I watched the story come to life. It is the story of two sets of sisters, Elaine and Adele from New Jersey, and Mildred and Betty from Kentucky. They made a pact that when they died they would meet up and visit retirement and assisted living communities.

Imagine my surprise—because in real life Elaine and Adele (sisters) were my aunts from New Jersey, and Betty (my mother) and Mildred (my aunt) were sisters from Kentucky! My Aunt Mildred was the last one to join The Patio Club. She passed away earlier in 2017. The Patio Club™ stories now touch people from around the country and hopefully someday from around the world.

My dream is that The Patio Club™ series will be read to the people in assisted living, memory and Hospice care communities. As I read each month to these special people, I realized that it is often difficult to visit loved ones who are in the assisted living population. What I have found is that reading a story seems to transform everyone from the reader to the listener. I have seen people with all kinds of health challenges perk up when listening to the joyful adventures of The Patio Club™. They are in the present moment as they listen and during that time there is nothing wrong with them.

My wish is that people will take the adventure of reading a story (about 12 to 15 minutes) from The Patio Club Series to a loved one. It will transform the visit from one where it may be difficult to find something to talk about, to one where both the reader and listener are moved beyond words.

With gratitude and love,

- Caryn

Acknowledgments

THE PATIO CLUB is dedicated to my aunts Elaine, Adele, Mildred, and my mother Betty. Although the characters in the Patio Club are fictional, they are based on these important women who impacted my life.

Special thanks to my sons Carson and Cooper, as well as, family and friends who have listened to these stories. They have enthusiastically cheered for me to follow my dream to write and illustrate stories that bring joy and adventure to the lives of others.

Finally, I am grateful to God for the gifts He has given me to serve the people in assisted living, memory and Hospice care.

About the Author

CARYN BEGAN WRITING children's stories for her children in the 1990s. In 2016, as she read children's stories to assisted living communities, residents asked her to write a story "for people their age." That was how the adventure of writing for the adult and assisted population began.

Since that time, Caryn has written a monthly series called The Patio Club®. It takes place at a retirement home/assisted living community named Happy Visions.

The Patio Club™ are the first stories published by Caryn for that age group. The stories have captured the attention of people of all ages across the country.

The Patio Club™ stories are a bridge between the reader and the listener. Family and friends that visit assisted living, memory and Hospice care communities may struggle for something to talk about. Reading a story like The Patio Club™ to these special residents takes them on an adventure without them ever having to leave the room. It creates an opening for some interesting conversations!

Caryn lives in Colorado. She has two grown sons, Carson and Cooper

www.ingramcontent.com/pod-product-compliance
Lightning Source LLC
Chambersburg PA
CBHW041609120626
46551CB00002B/366